SUZANNE SELFORS

WEDGIE & GIZMO

Illustrated by
Barbara Fisinger

KATHERINE TEGEN BOOKS
An Imprint of HarperCollinsPublishers

Katherine Tegen Books is an imprint of HarperCollins Publishers.

Wedgie & Gizmo
For information address HarperCollins Children's Books, a division
of HarperCollins Publishers, 195 Broadway, New York, NY 10007.
www.harpercollinschildrens.com
ISBN 978-0-06-244763-0
Typography by Carla Weise
17 18 19 20 21   CG/LSCH   10 9 8 7 6 5 4 3 2 1
❖
First Edition

To Faith Kerrigan
and her guinea pig, Spot—
both geniuses, but not
of the Evil variety.

FAMILY

Mom

Jasmine

Jackson

Wedgie

ALBUM

Abuela

Dad

Gizmo

Elliot

CHAPTER 1

Gizmo

GREETINGS TO YOU, DEAR READER. **MY NAME** is Gizmo. As you've probably heard, I am a genius. However, I am not a regular sort of genius, the kind who solves math problems or wins spelling bees. I am an Evil Genius, with an Evil Plan. Oh yes, it's true. A dastardly Evil Plan. But for now, my Evil Plan must wait, because I find myself in a most unpleasant situation.

No, I am not wedged in a drain. That happened once. One of my beloved marshmallows fell into the bathtub and I needed to get it. There was plenty of room in the pipe for my front half, but my back half is much rounder. Fortunately, my servant, Elliot, freed me. But alas, the marshmallow was never seen again.

No, I am not cornered by a hungry feline, or, as you might say, a *cat*. That also happened once. The cat crept in through a window and woke me from my mid-afternoon nap. Elliot was at school, so I had to save myself. I bonked the cat on the head with a toilet paper tube, then bit its nose. It never bothered me again.

So, though I am pleased to report that I am not stuck in a drain and not facing a hungry cat, what I face, at this very moment, is worse. Much worse!

I was forced to move to a new home! And it's pink!

How did this happen? I shall tell you. But be warned—it is not a nice story.

Yesterday, whilst enjoying an after-breakfast snack of carrot sticks, I was plucked from my Eco Habitat. Despite my squeals of protest, I was placed in a shoe box. After a lengthy journey, with neither a crumb to eat nor stick to chew, I awoke to find myself in a strange place.

No one asked *my opinion* about moving. No one gave me time to pack. And thus, all my hard work has been left behind. My tunnels. My treasures. My secret stash of marshmallows! I am irked, I tell you! Flustered! One day, when my Evil Plan is finished, all humans will feel my wrath!

But until that day, you may send your letters and care packages to my new address:

Gizmo the Evil Genius
The Barbie Playhouse
Atop the Bookcase in Jasmine's Room
Nowhere Near the Andes Mountains

Even though I have only been inside this horrid pink house for a few hours, I have gathered the following intelligence:

1. Barbie moved out of the playhouse and went to a land called Goodwill.
2. Though she left many pairs of plastic shoes, she will not be returning.
3. I am alone in this fiendish fortress.

Barbie's decision to move is understandable. There is no nest in the playhouse. No cave or laboratory. The plastic oven and plastic refrigerator do not work. And the plastic toilet does not flush. The only place for the elimination of waste is a container on the top floor.

JASMINE: Gross. Gizmo pooped in Barbie's bathtub.

ELLIOT: That's because you forgot to give him a litter box.

JASMINE: I'm so glad I get to take care of him.

ELLIOT: You only get to take care of him because his cage broke during the move. And because Dad said I'm supposed to be nice to you.

JASMINE: You have to be nice to me because I'm your new sister.
Don't worry. He'll be safe in my room.

ELLIOT: It's only for a little while. Just
until we buy him a new cage.
Remember, Gizmo belongs to me.

Until three days ago, Elliot was a loyal servant. He provided clean shredded newspaper, fresh water, and alfalfa pellets that were bland but contained a balanced ratio of vitamins to minerals. In addition, Elliot oiled my exercise wheel so it did not squeak and washed the windows in my Eco Habitat so I could enjoy the view. He gave me a pair of glasses so I could watch the nightly news from the comfort of my nest.

Elliot *never* tried to squeeze me into a tutu.

JASMINE: Doesn't he look cute?
ELLIOT: No, he doesn't look cute. He looks
ridiculous. Stop doing that.
JASMINE: But you said I could take care of
him.

ELLIOT: I never said you could put doll clothes on him. Besides, they're way too tight.

JASMINE: Well, it's not my fault he's shaped like a potato.

JACKSON: Ha-ha. He's a furry potato.

The new girl's name is Jasmine. I am not fond of her. I do not understand why she must pick me up and kiss me whenever she walks into the room. It is most unpleasant. And why must she carry me around in her pocket and sing songs to me? My time is valuable. I am an Evil Genius with important Evil Work to do!

MOM: Sweetie, don't you think you
should put the guinea pig down?

JASMINE: Gizmo likes being carried.

MOM: But he's grunting and biting your
finger.

JASMINE: That means he loves me. And I
love him sooooo much. He's the
sweetest guinea pig ever. I'm so
happy Elliot's letting Gizmo stay in
my room.

How many times must I tell these humans that the term *guinea pig* is incorrect? I am not from the *pig* family. I am a proud species of rodent belonging to the Caviidae family, and the genus *Cavia*. My species comes from the Andes Mountains, not from Guinea. But the humans insist on referring to me as a pig. Do I have a snout? No! Do I wallow in mud? No! How long must I bear these insults? Once I unleash my Evil Plan, they will never call me a pig again!

Which brings me to my updated list.

MY EVIL PLAN

1. Escape the pink prison and build an Evil Genius Lair.
2. Return Elliot to his rightful role as my servant.
3. Become the king of all cavies, create a cavy uprising, and take over the world!

Muh-ha-ha!

Alas, Jasmine is sticking me into her pocket again. Why must I suffer such humiliation?

CHAPTER 2

Wedgie

WHAT A GREAT DAY. I LOVE THIS DAY! I WISH every day could be like this day. I got half a waffle. And some toast crust. And a cup of kibble. I drank all the water from my bowl, I licked the shower floor, and I ate a dead fly. Now I'm standing at the door.

It's time to go on patrol. Hello? Let's go, people. Let's go outside!

MOM: Wedgie, stop barking!

My name's Wedgie, but my full name's Super Wedgie. I got that name because one night, a long time ago, Jasmine tied a red cape around my neck and took me to all the houses in the neighborhood. At each house I got a pat on the head, and Jasmine got treats that she put in a bag. There were lots of scary people wearing masks, but I barked at all of them and kept Jasmine safe. And when we got back home, I chased all the mask-wearing people out of our yard. The cape gave me superpowers! Now I wear it all the time. It helps me protect Jasmine and the rest of my pack.

There used to be three people in my pack—Mom and her two pups, Jasmine and Jackson. But my new dad and his pup, Elliot, moved in so now there are five people in my pack. It's my job to guard them from enemies and invaders. It's also my job to herd them so they don't get lost. It's a big job, but someone's gotta do it. And I'm that someone. Me. Super Wedgie!

What a great day. Let's go, people. Let's go outside!

DAD: Wedgie, stop scratching at the
door!

Super Wedgie has superpowers. If I run in a circle, again and again, with my cape flapping, I create an energized force field that opens the door. Ten times usually does the trick.

MOM: Oh for the love of Pete, will
someone take the dog for a walk?
JACKSON: I'll take him.
MOM: You're too little to take him. Elliot,
would you do it?
ELLIOT: Do I have to?
DAD: This is your chance to get to know
your new dog.

ELLIOT: But he's not my dog. He belongs to ... *them.*

DAD: He belongs to all of us. We're a family.

The force field is activated. The door opens!

I stand on the porch, my nose sniffing the air, my cape proudly displayed for all to see. Super Wedgie reporting for duty.

Elliot stands next to me. He smells like socks and syrup. I LOVE socks and syrup! And even though Elliot is new to my pack, I LOVE Elliot. He puts on the leash so I can take him for a walk.

Elliot needs the leash so he won't get lost. I gotta tug real hard to get Elliot moving. Come on, boy, let's go mark our territory!

Everyone in the neighborhood knows me. I'm real important around here. They all wave and talk to me as I pass by.

NEIGHBOR: Hey, don't pee on my roses!
DIFFERENT NEIGHBOR: Hey, stop chasing
                my cat!
DIFFERENT NEIGHBOR: Hey, you better
                scoop that poop!

Elliot puts my poop in a bag and carries it around. He must like the smell of poop as much as I do. And because I'm a superhero, my poop smells super poopy. I LOVE Elliot!

I lead Elliot around the block. I stop to smell Squirrel Tree. I stop to smell Raccoon Trail. I stop to smell Duck Pond. I know all the smells. That mushroom smells mushroomy. That pinecone smells pineconey. And that slime smells sluggy. We get close to home. I'm pulling as hard as I can. Jasmine is standing in our yard. I LOVE Jasmine! She smells like bubble gum and applesauce. But today she smells like something new. Hey! What's in Jasmine's pocket? I stick my nose inside. Oh wow, it's that Furry Potato. I LOVE the Furry Potato! I met him yesterday when he moved into Jasmine's room and that means he's under my protection, just like the rest of my pack. He's very nice and very squeaky. I'm standing on my hind legs.

I'm wagging my stubby tail. Please oh please oh please let me smell the Furry Potato.

ELLIOT: Why did you bring Gizmo outside?
JASMINE: I'm showing him around the neighborhood. Look, Gizmo, here's your new driveway and your new mailbox. And your new dog.

ELLIOT: Watch out! It looks like Wedgie
wants to eat him.
JASMINE: Wedgie would never eat Gizmo.
Wedgie just wants to be friends.

I sniff him all over. I smell his face, his
ears, his paws, and his rump. Furry Potato
smells like the inside of Jasmine's pocket.
I get fur in my nose. I sneeze. The Furry
Potato grunts and squeaks at me. I don't
speak potato, but I know he's telling me that
he LOVES me as much as I LOVE him. He's
my new friend.

Never worry, Furry Potato. Super Wedgie's
on duty, day and night, night and day, to
protect the pack, come what—

CAT!

ELLIOT: Wedgie, come back!

CHAPTER 3

Gizmo

YESTERDAY, WHEN WE ARRIVED AT THIS house, I made a shocking discovery. These new humans own a canine, or, as you might say, a *dog*. And they allow him to live inside. He is a four-legged, drooling beast of questionable intelligence. He wears a cape and sticks his nose everywhere, including my backside. How rude! If he continues this behavior, he shall feel my wrath. But until then, I have important matters to deal with.

My goal today is to explore the world

outside the Barbie Playhouse. It is well known that every Evil Genius has an Evil Lair, so if I am to build one, then I will need to find the perfect location. This pink playhouse simply will not do.

But the human girl named Jasmine continues to bother me, so I burrow deep in my nest. Does she not see the appointment calendar taped to the front door? It clearly states that I am busy.

> Sign up here if you want an appointment
> with Gizmo the Evil Genius.

When Jasmine tries to pet me, I let her know that I am not in the mood for cuddling!

JASMINE: Ow! Gizmo bit me again. How come he bit me?

MOM: He's not used to you yet. Give him time. Let's go get a bandage.

As soon as the humans leave the room, I collect a Polar Expedition Rucksack, another item Barbie left behind. She must be an explorer. I fill the rucksack with the necessary survival items—a bottle of water and some carrot sticks. I open the front door of the playhouse, step out, and gaze upon my surroundings.

The Barbie Playhouse is perched atop a bookcase, giving me a sweeping view. Beneath the window is the girl's nest—a jumbled mountain of blankets and pillows. Though this room offers many nooks and crannies, it would not be a good location for my Evil Lair. Too many interruptions. Believe me, that Jasmine is trouble. Earlier, she pulled me from my second morning nap for some kind of strange ritual.

JASMINE: Would you like a cup of tea?
You're just the cutest thing ever!

I need to explore the rest of this human house, but the exit lies on the opposite end of the room. To reach it, I must cross a landscape littered with plastic building blocks, terrible-tasting wax crayons, and large furry creatures with eyes that never blink.

Though I know how to build a lever and pulley system that would lower me to the ground, there is no time to waste. Those humans could return at any moment.

So, with great risk to myself, I close my eyes and leap. I am happy to report a safe landing in a basket of human clothing.

After climbing out of the basket, I make sure my Polar Expedition Rucksack is secure. Then I look around. The terrain is not for the faint of heart. I make my way through a maze of limbs and frozen faces. I am almost crushed by a tower of blocks and nearly overcome by a smelly sock. Fortunately, I find a treat along the way. It is a circular item known as a Cheerio and is quite crunchy. I decide to take a short break to refuel. Then I find a freeze-ray gun and some clever disguises. I stuff these items into my rucksack.

Alas, to my dismay, my ears catch the sound of footsteps. The human girl child is returning! You may have heard, dear reader, that I am a master of disguise. Back in my youth, when I lived at Swampy's Pet Shop, my cage neighbor was a chameleon who

taught me everything she knew. "Blend in," she told me. "That's the trick." So, as the footsteps grew closer, I hid. Jasmine would never find me!

JASMINE: Gizmo! What are you doing? Uh-oh, he's stuck. I can't get him out. Help!

CHAPTER 4

Wedgie

WHAT'S THAT? SOMEONE'S CALLING FOR HELP!
Help is a very important word that every superhero must pay attention to. Other important words are *stay* and *sit*. *Get* is also important, like "*Get* off the couch," or "*Get* outta the pantry." There's *stop*, like "*Stop* chewing on that shoe" or "*Stop* rolling on that stinky thing." Another big word is *don't*—"*Don't* eat that garbage," "*Don't* chase that cat," and "*Don't* drink out of the toilet."

But right now the word is *help* and it's

Jasmine who needs me. I stop chewing on the new boy's sock and I race down the hall. The floor's super slippery. I bonk into the wall. Maybe if I skid on my belly, I can get there faster. Super Wedgie to the rescue!

I hurry into Jasmine's bedroom. Super Wedgie is here! Ready to save the day! Jasmine's shaking something up and down. She shakes and shakes and the something flies through the air and lands on Jasmine's bed. I'll get it! Her bed's much taller than me, but I use my special doggy stairs. Oh, how I LOVE Jasmine's bed. It's soft and it

smells like Cheerios and shampoo. I find one Cheerio, then another Cheerio. She's left them for me. She's so nice.

I crawl through the blankets, sniffing for more Cheerios. Then I find something else.

It's furry and it's grunting.

Why, it's the Furry Potato. What are you doing in Jasmine's bed, Furry Potato? You aren't supposed to be here. Did you fall out of your house? That's not very smart. I sniff him all over. He sure makes funny noises. He must LOVE me as much as I LOVE him. Using my nose, I push him across the bed. Jasmine, look what I found!

JASMINE: There you are, you silly little guinea pig. I'd better put you back where you belong.
Thanks for finding him, Wedgie.

I jump off the bed and watch while Jasmine puts the Furry Potato in his house. Then she scratches behind my ear. And my other ear. That feels so good. She scratches my rump. I LOVE it when she scratches my rump. I'm a very happy dog.

ELLIOT: What's that?

JASMINE: It's the Biju Ting Ting Scalp Massager.

ELLIOT: It's for your scalp? So why are you using it on Wedgie's rump?

JASMINE: He likes it.

ELLIOT: Why does he always wear that cape?

JASMINE: I gave it to him for Halloween last year. He looks so cute in it.

MOM: Wedgie? Do you want a bone?

Bone? Oh, that's another very important word. Yes, I want a bone! I want a bone real bad! I run out of Jasmine's room. My legs are moving as fast as they can. I slip and slide around the corner, then bound across the kitchen floor. I can smell it. It smells good. I lick my lips. I start to drool. Gimme that bone! Oh please oh please oh please gimme that bone!

Mom gives it to me. It's a good bone, with

marrow in the middle. I LOVE this bone!

Using my superpowers, I run in five circles. Force field activated! The front door opens. I'm outside with my bone. There's only one thing to do. I must bury it and wait until it is ripe.

I'm gonna bury it under Squirrel Tree because that's my favorite place. I dig as fast as I can. The ground is soft. I find a root and tuck the bone under it. Then I cover the bone with dirt. I piddle on the tree so everyone knows it's mine. I'll check on the bone every day. Sometimes I forget where I bury my bones, but not this time. This is my favorite bone and I'll protect it. And when it gets ripe, I'll eat it. I LOVE this bone.

But what's that sound? I whip around. Brutus is lying in his yard, behind the fence. He's watching me. He wants my bone. But he can't have it. This is my bone, Brutus! And this is my stick! And this is my ball!

DAD: Why is Wedgie barking at that old
dog?

MOM: Wedgie barks at everything. But
Brutus is so old, he can't hear
Wedgie. He's totally deaf.

ELLIOT: Is Brutus sleeping with his eyes half
open?

MOM: Yep. It drives Wedgie crazy.

That's right, Brutus, you stay over there,
on your side of the fence. You don't want to
mess with me, Super Wedgie. I've got my

pack to protect, like my new boy and my new dad. I circle around my new dad and he pets me. Then I circle around Elliot. But Elliot doesn't reach down. Why won't Elliot pet me?

DAD: What's wrong, Elliot? You seem upset.

ELLIOT: I don't like it here. I don't have any friends.

DAD: It's not easy moving to a new place. But when school starts next month, you'll make new friends.

ELLIOT: I don't want new friends. I want my old friends.

Elliot's voice sounds sad. Why's Elliot sad? Is Brutus making him sad? Is he worried that Brutus is going to take my bone?

Hey, Brutus! I see you staring at me. I'm not afraid of you, Brutus. You'll never have my bone. I'll guard it with my life! And I'll

guard my stick. And my ball. And my family!

Super Wedgie's on duty, day and night, night and day, to protect the pack, come what—

SQUIRREL!

CHAPTER 5

Gizmo

IT IS MY SECOND NIGHT INSIDE THE BARBIE Playhouse. I am sorry to say that I have made no progress toward building my new Evil Lair. Each time I attempt an expedition, the girl and the canine get in my way. But this time will be different, for I shall wait for darkness. Then, as soon as everyone has fallen asleep, I will make my escape.

Whilst I wait, I decide to redecorate. These pink walls irk me to my core!

I make a bigger nest. I make some tunnels. And I add more carpeting. Interior design is one of my many talents.

MOM: Lights out.

JASMINE: Please please please let me read a little bit more.

MOM: You know the rules. It's time for sleep, sweetie.

What's Gizmo doing over there?

DAD: He likes to build things with toilet paper rolls.

JASMINE: He's so silly.

Night, Mom. Night, Dad.

DAD: She called me *Dad*.

As soon as the adult humans leave the room, I step onto the balcony, watching and waiting for the girl to fall asleep. She is tucked deep into her nest. Soon her breathing slows. I hear the sounds of doors closing and the entire house falls into silence. My time has come! I climb out of the playhouse and jump into the basket of clothing. I am determined to succeed. World domination cannot begin without a new Evil Lair.

You may be curious, dear reader, about

my old Evil Lair. It was hidden behind a machine called Maytag Dryer. It was warm back there, with lots of lint balls for nest-making. An Evil Genius needs to take at least five naps a day, so a comfortable nest is one of the most important parts of a lair. The site also provided plenty of privacy for writing letters to Gweneviere. Gweneviere is a tri-colored, long-haired cavy who lived across the aisle from me at Swampy's Pet Shop. Oh, how I loved watching her waddle on her wheel. A true athlete. A waddling champion! One day, whilst Gweneviere was in the middle of a training session, Elliot came to

the pet shop and offered to be my human servant. As he carried me away I called out to Gweneviere—"When I rule the world, you shall be my queen!" I have been writing letters to her ever since, so that she knows my plans are

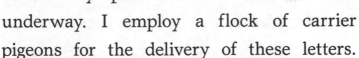

underway. I employ a flock of carrier pigeons for the delivery of these letters.

I pay them in sunflower seeds.

One day, Gweneviere and I shall waddle, side by side, in a glorious world where cavies roam free, and where all humans serve us!

But until that day, I have work to accomplish. And thus, I scurry across Jasmine's room, locate the Polar Expedition Rucksack, which is lying next to a shoe, and make my way toward the exit. I stop for a moment, listening for sounds that the canine might be up and about. It is quiet. That drooling beast is asleep somewhere. I shall do my best to avoid him.

Because we cavies are soft and round and low to the ground, we can move across floors as silently as lint balls. I traverse the length of the hall without interruption, stopping at the first open door. I peer inside. Elliot is asleep in his nest. I shall need to have a conversation with him about his servant duties. He has been most forgetful. My litter box is not as clean as it should be. And my treat bowl was empty on two occasions! This is not acceptable. We Evil Geniuses need a constant supply of food to fuel our Evil Genius Brains!

The room in which Elliot sleeps might be an excellent place for my new Evil Lair. However, I would like to see the rest of the house. So I continue down the hallway. A loud noise greets me as I turn the corner. My tiny heart begins to pound. The canine! My legs stiffen, ready to run, but then I realize that the canine's eyes are closed. He is lying on his side, snoring, with a puddle of drool beneath his mouth. His front legs twitch. Is he dreaming? I doubt that a creature with such little intelligence can dream, but if he can, I suspect they are dreams about silly things, like chasing his own stubby tail or barking at his own shadow. Nothing like my dreams, which are big, and important, and Evil.

His inferior brain does not detect me as I scurry past.

A trail of scents leads me to the room where the humans prepare their meals. Beyond another door I find a supply of food that is stacked from the floor to the ceiling. Never in my life have I seen so many edibles. And there, on the first shelf, I spy boxes of cereal, one of the most wondrous of foods. It will be easy for me to reach them. We cavies have very strong legs and mine are extra strong, thanks to Gweneviere. She inspires me to work out on my wheel, in between my naps and my Evil Plan-making. The Barbie Playhouse does not have a wheel. This is another thing I shall need to discuss with Elliot.

I jump onto the first shelf and begin to chew a hole in a box. Oh, what delicious treats will I find inside? My rump wiggles with excitement. But it is crowded on that shelf, and my wiggling causes the box to fall to the floor. Upon impact it opens, spilling its glorious contents. There are shapes—pink hearts, green clovers, and yellow stars. I prick my tiny ears, worried that the noise has alerted the canine. But he continues to snore. The feast is mine!

I jump off the shelf and nibble on a yellow star. Joy of joys! It is marshmallow, my most favorite treat in the entire world! I am not supposed to eat them. Elliot says they will make me sick. But I cannot resist. They are scrumptious! I dig through the whole box, eating as many as I can find.

Just as I swallow the last shape, sunlight peeks through the kitchen window. Morning has arrived. I need to get back to Jasmine's room before my escape is discovered. And I have a new goal to add to my list. Once I take over the world, I shall make certain that cavies everywhere have as many pink hearts, green clovers, and yellow stars as they desire. I shall make marshmallow shapes the official food of all cavies!

I start waddling down the hallway, but it is difficult to move. There is a strange feeling in my belly.

JASMINE: Mom! Dad! Something's wrong with Gizmo. His tummy is huge!

ELLIOT: What did you do to him?

JASMINE: I didn't do anything to him. I love him!

JACKSON: Gizmo just farted.

JASMINE: I didn't know guinea pigs could fart.

ELLIOT: Dad, he looks sick. What should we do?

CHAPTER 6

Wedgie

HEY, SOMEONE LEFT A BOX OF CEREAL ON THE floor. What a great way to start the morning. I LOVE people food. Any kind of people food. Bread, noodles, cookies. Hot dogs are the best. Turkey's good too. Ice cream makes me shiver but I LOVE it. This cereal is super crunchy. I'm gonna eat it as fast as I can. I don't even have to chew. The little pieces stick right to my tongue. Wow, this tastes really good! Hey, how come it smells like the Furry Potato in here?

MOM: Wedgie! Bad dog! Get outta the
pantry.

Uh-oh. I'm a bad dog. I take one more bite before the pantry door closes. Why am I a bad dog? The cereal was on the floor. I like to eat things that are on the floor. I wag my stubby tail again. Pet me pet me pet me and tell me I'm a good dog.

But Mom doesn't pet me. She grabs my leash. She wants me to take her on a walk. Sure thing. I LOVE to take Mom on a walk! We go outside. I piddle on the hedge. I bark at Brutus. Stay away from my bone, Brutus! Then I try to piddle on Squirrel Tree, but Mom pulls me to the car. The whole family's in the car. The Furry Potato's in the car, too. I LOVE going for car rides. Dad lifts me inside and I sit on Jasmine's lap. Where are we going? Are we going to the park? I press my nose to the window. Yep, we're going to the park. Here comes the park. There it is.

Hey, how come we didn't stop at the park? I walk onto Jackson's lap. I try to walk onto Elliot's lap, but he pushes me away. He's holding the Furry Potato. The Furry Potato smells different today. He smells like cereal. I LOVE cereal! I walk back to Jasmine. I press my nose to the window again. Are we going to Dog Beach? Yep, we're going to Dog Beach. Here comes Dog Beach. There it is.

Hey, how come we didn't stop at the beach? Where are we going, people?

The car stops. Oh no. Not that place. No no no no no! I'm shaking all over. Don't take me into THAT place! I jump to the floor and try to hide under Jackson's feet. No no no no no! I don't want to go to THAT place!

MOM: Wedgie, stop whining. You're not seeing the vet. Gizmo is seeing the vet.

JASMINE: Yeah, because he got really fat.

JACKSON: And he's farting.

ELLIOT: Jasmine fed him something bad.

JASMINE: No, I didn't. I promise.

DAD: Come on, kids, let's go inside and see what the doctor says.

Now Mom's holding my leash. I crawl under the car. I use all my super strength so she can't pull me. But my new dad reaches under and picks me up. He carries me inside.

This place is a terrible place. It smells like fear and sadness. A dog's whimpering in the corner. A cat's howling from its box. I must warn them. RUN! I tell them. RUN as fast as you can from this place. And whatever you do, don't go into one of those rooms. They do terrible things to you in those rooms. They poke you in the rump, and they stick you with needles. They put drops in your ears and bad-tasting pills in your mouth. Come, follow me! We'll escape together! I run in a circle five times, but my force field doesn't activate.

The door doesn't open. My superpowers don't work here. This place is bad. Very very bad.

VET : Okay, we can see Gizmo now. Come on in.

ELLIOT: He's my pet. I'll take him.

JASMINE: But I want to come too.

ELLIOT: Haven't you done enough already?

JASMINE: Mom, why is Elliot so mad at me?

MOM: Elliot's just worried, sweetie. He's having a hard time right now.

JASMINE: I didn't feed Gizmo anything bad. I promise.

MOM: I know you didn't.

Don't go into that room, Furry Potato! The door closes. What are they doing in there? I sniff along the floor. I sniff under the chairs. I sniff along the wall. I sniff all the shoes. I peek into the cat's box. I see you, cat. Listen to me, cat. When you go into that room, it's gonna be bad. Real bad! The cat blinks at me. I look at the other dog. We're both shivering. We're both looking out the window. Can we go outside? Please oh please oh please? I scratch the door. Can we get out of this bad place?

Be brave, Furry Potato! I holler. Be brave!

CHAPTER 7

Gizmo

ELLIOT IS HOLDING ME IN HIS HANDS, WHICH are warm but not as soft as my nest. I wish I were in my nest. Strange sounds are coming from my belly. Churning and rumbling, like a storm. I fear I am doomed. Will this be the end of Gizmo the Evil Genius? Get me a pen and paper, Elliot, so that I may write a farewell to my beloved Gweneviere. Open a window, so that I may summon a pigeon to carry my good-bye. I open my mouth to tell Elliot these things, but I am too weak to squeak.

Alas, what a tragedy! The cavies are waiting for me to become their king. To rule their cavy world. But if I perish, they will never have a king. They will never know the glory of leaving their cages and living free!

My belly makes another disturbing sound. What has happened to me? I was eating those delicious marshmallow shapes and then I was struck down with some kind of sickness. It is a mystery that not even my Evil Genius Mind can solve. Perhaps I caught a virus from that drooling canine. He sticks his nose into everything, and then he sticks it on me, spreading who knows what kind of germs. Yes, this is his fault!

Elliot carries me into a smaller room. I feel so bad. My tummy gurgles.

ELLIOT: Dad, I'm worried. Gizmo looks terrible.

DAD: He'll be okay. The doctor will be here soon.

EXERCISE YOUR DOG

AT LEAST TWENTY MINUTES A DAY

I look around. There are posters on the walls. One reads *Exercise Your Dog at Least Twenty Minutes a Day.* What is wrong with dogs? Why can't they exercise themselves?

Another reads *Don't Feed People Food to Your Pets.* That doesn't seem fair. Why don't humans want to share their food?

I have many questions, but I am too sick to talk. I roll over in Elliot's hands. I close my eyes and begin to dream that I am back at Swampy's Pet Shop. That is where I learned to read. Mr. Swampy had a parrot, and he spent an hour each morning teaching the alphabet to

DON'T FEED PEOPLE FOOD TO YOUR PETS.

this parrot. I listened, for it was very interesting. It only took me a couple of days to learn the alphabet, and soon I was able to spell out words. It was then I discovered that the lining of my cage was covered in interesting articles. I began to read. I enjoyed the restaurant reviews. I also liked the classified ads, where you could buy everything from furniture to cars. Even animals were for sale. I was horrified to learn that we cavies cost much less than canines. Why would a human pay more for a *dog*? How troubling. I read the articles quickly, then I asked the chameleon to read me his. But I discovered that he could not read. In fact, none of the other animals could read. They did not gather information from their cage linings— they just pooped on them.

I was unique. Different. That is when I realized that I was a genius.

I wanted to share my talent with Gweneviere. Whilst she waddled on her wheel,

I read aloud to her, helping her learn how to spell out words. I had to speak loudly, over the constant chirping of the lovebirds and croaking of the frogs. I tried to give a reading lesson every day. Gweneviere never read back to me, but that is because she was so busy with her training. I know she learned. Who better to teach her than an actual Genius? Oh, how I do miss her.

I open my eyes. Another human has entered the room.

DR. PINE: Hello. I'm Doctor Pine. What's your guinea pig's name?

ELLIOT: His name is Gizmo.

DR. PINE: He's very overweight. What have you been feeding him?

ELLIOT: Timothy hay, alfalfa pellets, carrots, and apples. And broccoli.

DR. PINE: Those are the right things.

DAD: But he got loose, so he might have eaten something else.

DR. PINE: Please put him on the table and I'll take a look.

Elliot places me on a cold metal table. I shiver. Then the doctor presses something against my tummy. Alas, what torture is this? I try to bite her, but she is quick. Oh foul creature, leave me alone!

She does not obey. Instead, she announces that she is going to give me an X-ray. I have read about these devices. In Elliot's comic books, X-ray beams are shot at Evil Villains to disintegrate them! I must make my escape! When the doctor picks me up, I try to pry open her fingers with my nose, but her grip is tight. I squeak. I grunt. I poop in her hand. But she does not care. She carries me into another room and sets me in a basin. The sides are slippery. I cannot climb to freedom. She steps away. A humming sound fills the air. A light flashes. I hold my breath. Is this the end of Gizmo?

The humming stops. The light is gone. The doctor scoops me out of the basin and carries me back to Elliot. I am alive! I am too Evil for the X-ray device! I groan with relief. I also groan because my tummy still hurts.

DR. PINE: I think this is a case of indigestion.

ELLIOT: Is he going to die?

DR. PINE: No. But he definitely ate too much.

Ate too much? I prick my ears. It is not possible for a cavy to eat too much. Eating is what we do! This doctor doesn't know what she's talking about. I have always been proud of my eating. Why, at Swampy's Pet Shop, I was famous for my appetite. One night, using a chewing stick, I pried open the door to my cage and waddled along the shelf until I came to a glorious display called *Treats for Rodents*. I was enchanted by the choices—seed and nut clusters, fruit wafers, and golden corncobs. For a moment I wished I were a hamster, able to stuff my cheek pockets and take the goodies back to my cage. I spent the whole night eating, resting only for three naps. Mrs. Swampy found me in the morning, asleep on a pile of wrappers. "Oh, you little Evil Genius," she said to me. And that is when I discovered the truth. I wasn't just a genius.

I was an *Evil Genius*.

Elliot is picking me up again. His hands feel so nice and warm after that cold metal table. But my belly still hurts.

DR. PINE: Keep him on a strict diet of alfalfa and water for a few days.

DAD: Thank you, doctor.

ELLIOT: Thank you.

DR. PINE: Good-bye, Elliot and Mr. Washington. Good-bye, Gizmo.

Good riddance to you, doctor! How dare you poke at me and tell me I eat too much. You know nothing about cavies! When I recover, you shall feel my wrath!

CHAPTER 8

Wedgie

MY NEW DAD, AND ELLIOT, AND THE FURRY Potato have been inside that room for a long time. I'm shivering. And panting. I've smelled everyone's ankles. I've talked to every dog and cat. I walk back and forth, from one end of the room to the other, as far as my leash will go. I feel very bad and I really want to get out of here.

MOM: Wedgie, calm down.

JASMINE: Mom, do you think Gizmo will be okay?

MOM: Well, let's think positive thoughts.

JASMINE: I didn't let him out of his cage.

MOM: I know, sweetie.

JACKSON: Wedgie is going crazy!

Something's happening! Dad and Elliot come out of that bad room. Elliot's holding the Furry Potato. I wag my tail. Are we done? Can we go home? But then I see the lady who wears the white coat. I'm scared of her. I scoot under a chair to hide from the lady with the white coat. But as soon as she leaves, I dart out and run to the door. It's time to make our escape! Let's go, people!

I run in circles in front of the door. Come on, superpowers. Work! I run and run. The door opens! Yes! Super Wedgie to the rescue. We leave the place that smells like sadness and fear. I tug on my leash, pulling Dad toward our car. Everyone gets in. Dad lifts me and puts me onto Jasmine's lap. I lick Jasmine's face. I'm so happy that we're going home. I LOVE home.

MOM: So, what did the doctor say?

DAD: He said that Gizmo ate something bad and got indigestion. We need to keep him on a healthy diet.

JACKSON: Gizmo's farts smell like cereal.

ELLIOT: He could have died. I'm not letting Jasmine take care of him anymore!

DAD: This isn't your sister's fault.

ELLIOT: She's not my sister.

The car begins to drive. Jasmine wraps her arms around me and squeezes. I lick a tear off Jasmine's face. Don't be sad, Jasmine. Super Wedgie opened the door and got us out of that bad place. We're going home!

CHAPTER 9

Gizmo

HELLO AGAIN, DEAR READER. I AM PLEASED TO report that I have convinced Elliot to return to his role as my faithful servant. Yesterday, after that unpleasant visit to the doctor's office, Elliot moved the Barbie Playhouse to his room. This is a welcome change. Elliot does not carry me in his pocket or sing songs to me. He does not dress me in sparkly clothing or sprinkle glitter into my house. Because of my seven days in Jasmine's room, there is glitter in my poop.

I cannot rule the world with glittery poop!

But alas, even though I have left Jasmine's room, she still bothers me. Elliot posted a large sign on his door that reads **STAY OUT**, but Jasmine ignores it. This morning, she brought a device into his room, the likes of which I have never before seen. It is called the Biju Ting Ting Scalp Massager. When she places it over my backside, waves of relaxation roll up my spine. My eyes close and a strange purring sound comes from my throat. I fall into a trance and cannot move. This device could be used by my enemies to cntrap me. It must be destroyed! I shall do so as soon as possible.

But for now, until further notice, please address your letters and care packages to me at:

Gizmo the Evil Genius
The Barbie Playhouse
Atop Elliot's Bookcase
Nowhere Near the Andes Mountains

ELLIOT: Don't worry, Gizmo. I know moving is hard. But I'm here and I won't let anyone else take care of you ever again.

DAD: Hey, Elliot, I just got an email about Gizmo's new cage. It'll be here in a week.

ELLIOT: A week? That's a long time.

DAD: Those Eco Habitats are really popular.

As I wake from my noon nap, I yawn and stretch. My belly is starting to feel better, but my energy level is low. After eating alfalfa pellets and drinking water, I consider taking another nap, but I notice that Elliot is sitting on the carpet, reading his comic books. I am in the mood to read, so I squeak at Elliot. He picks me up and sets me next to him. I search through the stack and find a story about a superhero named Thor.

I have read many of Elliot's comic books. It would appear that every Evil Genius has a rival—a superhero who gets in the way and tries to ruin the Evil Genius's Evil Plan. I consider this as I nibble a corner of the book. I am an Evil Genius, so why do I not have a superhero who is trying to ruin my Evil Plan? If I am to be taken seriously, I *must* have an enemy superhero! Where can I find one? This is of the utmost importance. I update my list.

MY EVIL PLAN

1. Escape the pink prison and build an Evil Genius Lair.
2. Find an enemy superhero.
3. Make pink hearts, green clovers, and yellow stars the official food of all cavies.
4. Become the king of all cavies, create a cavy uprising, and take over the world!

The canine enters the room. Drat! He ambles toward me, panting.

I tuck my nose under the comic book because dog breath is horrid! I try to hide, but he roots beneath the pages until he finds me, then he sniffs me all over. So rude! *Be gone,* I tell him. *Go away!* But instead of leaving, he begins to run circles around me. Why is he engaging in this activity? He is so very bothersome.

MOM: How are you guys doing?

ELLIOT: Why does Wedgie always run around Gizmo?

MOM: He's a Welsh corgi. His instinct is to herd.

ELLIOT: Herd?

MOM: Yes. Corgis are bred to herd livestock on farms. Like goats and sheep.

ELLIOT: But Gizmo's not a sheep. And this isn't a farm.

MOM: He's just trying to make sure that Gizmo doesn't get lost. Come on, Wedgie, let's get a treat.

He thinks I am livestock? The canine has insulted me for the final time! I must come up with an Evil Plan to rid myself of him. But that is when I notice something. As the canine dashes out of the room, his red cape flaps. A shiver darts down my spine. I look at the comic book. The canine's red cape is the same cape that Thor wears. Does this mean what I think it means?

Yes! The corgi canine is my enemy superhero, sent to destroy me.

He is Thorgi!

CHAPTER 10

Wedgie

I'M GETTING A TREAT! A TREAT! A TREAT!
Give me that treat.
Give me that treat
right now. I
want it. I
want that
treat!

Oh boy, I
just got a treat!

CHAPTER **11**

Gizmo

DEAR READER, IF YOU REMEMBER, I JUST DIS-
covered that the corgi canine is actually
Thorgi, a superhero dog who has been sent
to defeat me. Now everything makes sense.
This is why we moved to this new house.
So that I could face my archenemy nose to
nose. How delightful. His primitive brain
will be no match for my super intelligence.
He will prove easy to beat.

Muh-ha-ha.

In order to concoct a cunning plan to

defeat Thorgi, I will need to do some research, so I continue to read the Thor comic book. That is when I find an interesting advertisement.

Thor's hammer? What a glorious discovery! According to Elliot's comic book, Thor's hammer is a most powerful tool, and it could be mine! I tremble at the thought. All I have to do is fill out the form and send it to the

proper address. Then the hammer will be delivered and after one bonk, I will be rid of my archenemy!

Using my sharp teeth, I chew around the edges of the order form. Then, gripping it in my mouth, I carry it under Elliot's desk, where I find a pen. I begin to fill out the form. When I am done, I carry the form across the room. Then I stand below the Barbie Playhouse and grunt.

ELLIOT: Do you want back into your house?

Elliot places me in the Barbie Playhouse. As he grabs another comic book to read, I waddle along his bookcase until I come to the window. It is cracked open. I slide the order form through the crack, leaving it on the outside windowsill. One of my carrier pigeons will arrive and deliver it, of this I am certain. They are very loyal pigeons. I must find a new supply of sunflower seeds so that I can reward them for their service.

> **JASMINE:** Come on, Elliot. It's time for *Peru Today*.
> **ELLIOT:** What's *Peru Today*?
> **JASMINE:** It's Abuela's favorite show. She wants us to watch it with her.

Did I hear the word *Peru*? My ears prick. Peru is the native homeland of cavies. Why are these humans talking about it? Elliot picks me up. He carries me down the hallway. Is he taking me to the room with the marshmallow shapes? I squeak eagerly. But he passes that room, and instead, carries me into a room with a large television mounted on the wall. I enjoy television. Especially the nightly news. A future Evil Ruler must keep up with current events.

Elliot sits on the carpet and that is when I make another important discovery. There is an elderly human who lives in the house.

They call her Abuela. I observe her for a few minutes. Like me, she wears glasses. Like me, she issues orders and her human servants obey. She appears to have a throne.

> **ABUELA:** Get me my cheese puffs. It's time to watch my show!
> **ELLIOT:** How come you like this show?
> **ABUELA:** Because I'm from Peru. Now shhh. It's starting.

Imagine my joy to learn that I was in the presence of someone who came from Peru, the cavy homeland. The land of the Andes Mountains. The land where cavies run free. Was this another reason why I had been brought to this new house? So that the Elderly One can become one of my minions? Of course! She is from Peru and thus she is a friend to all cavies. Of this, I am certain.

And what great luck that we are going to watch a television show about Peru—the

very place where I will one day build my Evil Castle and rule supreme with my queen, Gweneviere.

I settle on a cushion, my gaze on the television screen. Oh, how glorious to see the snow-capped mountains. And to see herds of cavies in their natural habitat, eating sweet grass. I can practically smell the crisp mountain air.

My keen eyesight picks up movement. A cheese puff falls from the Elderly One's hand. Eating nothing but alfalfa pellets has been torture. I grab the delicacy and burrow beneath a pillow to enjoy my lovely prize. But just as I am about to sink my teeth into the crunchy treat, the canine's big wet nose invades my space. With a quick swoop of his tongue, the treat disappears. No! I holler. How dare you take my cheese puff! You vile beast! When the Hammer of Thor arrives, you shall feel my wrath!

JASMINE: Why is Gizmo squeaking?

ELLIOT: Wedgie's trying to eat him!

JASMINE: Wedgie would never do that.

ELLIOT: Hey, did that lady on the TV just say they eat guinea pigs in Peru?

ABUELA: Yes.

JASMINE: Why would they do that? Guinea pigs are too cute to eat!

ABUELA: In Peru, guinea pigs are food. Not pets.

JACKSON: I don't wanna eat Gizmo.

What was that? Did I hear what I think I heard? I emerge from the pillow. Everyone is staring at me. I turn my attention to the television show and I see something so vile, it shocks me to my very core.

CHAPTER 12

Wedgie

HOW COME FURRY POTATO GETS TO SIT ON the couch? I never get to sit on the couch. It's a good thing I found Furry Potato under the pillow. He was lost again. Silly Furry Potato.

Jasmine's fingers are covered in orange stuff. I lick her fingers. I LOVE orange stuff. Elliot still doesn't pet me. I lick his hand but he pushes me away. Why is Elliot so sad?

Everyone is watching the television screen. I don't like the television screen. When my family stares at it, they don't pet me.

Hey, what's that sound? I run to the door. I sniff the crack under the door. Oh no! Brutus is out there! Red alert, red alert, Brutus is in the yard! I run back to the living room. Hey, Brutus is in the yard. Keep the pups inside. Hide under the bed. People, stop looking at the television and pay attention to me. Are you listening?

ABUELA: Wedgie, stop barking. I can't hear my show.

JASMINE: Wedgie wants to go outside.

ELLIOT: I'll go outside with him. I don't really like this show, anyway. All that talk about eating guinea pigs is scaring Gizmo.

Don't worry, Elliot. There's no need to be sad. I'll chase Brutus from our yard. Elliot is carrying the Furry Potato in his hands. I herd them toward the door. Then I circle in front of the door, engaging my superpowers.

Let me out let me out let me out. The force field is activated and the door opens.

Brutus! I holler. My cape flies behind me as I run down the walkway. Then I skid to a stop. Brutus is on the other side of the fence, in his yard. He makes a circle, then lies down. I know you were here, I tell him. I sniff the hedge. Brutus piddled on it, so I piddle on it. I sniff Squirrel Tree. Brutus piddled on it, so I piddle on it. I check the bone. It's safe. I check the ball and the stick. They're safe, but the stick smells like Brutus. He touched my stick?

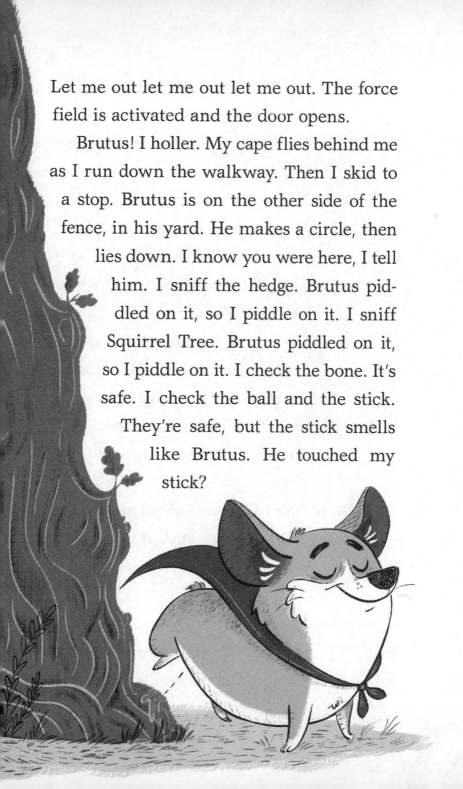

ELLIOT: Hey, Dad, I just watched this weird show with Jasmine's grandmother. Did you know they eat guinea pigs in Peru?

DAD: They do?

ELLIOT: Abuela is from Peru. Do you think she wants to eat Gizmo?

DAD: Ha-ha. No, I don't think you have to worry about that.
The only thing you need to worry about is your birthday. Have you decided what you'd like to do?

ELLIOT: I want to invite my old friends.

DAD: I'm sorry, Elliot, but they're too far away.

ELLIOT: Then I don't care about my birthday. (Elliot kicks the stick. It flies over the fence.)

My stick! I need my stick. I run along the fence. I jump and jump and jump but I can't get over the fence. I stick my head between

the fence posts and push with my back legs.
Don't touch my stick! I tell Brutus. I push
and push and push.

Uh-oh. I'm stuck.

DAD, freeing Wedgie from the fence: Wedgie,
  you're acting crazy. What's the matter
  with you?
  Brutus is too old to play with you.

I was stuck but now I'm free. I want to get my stick but something catches my eye. What's this? A piece of paper's floating in the air. It lands in my yard. Do you see, Brutus? This is my piece of paper. I grab it with my teeth. Then I dig a hole beneath Squirrel Tree and bury the piece of paper where it'll be safe. I cover it with dirt. Then I piddle on the spot so Brutus knows it's mine.

I walk over to Elliot. I press my nose against his ankle. Elliot still won't pet me. Is he sad because my stick is gone? I'll wait for the gate to open. And then I will get my stick. And then Elliot will be happy.

CHAPTER 13

Gizmo

DEAR READER, YOU MAY WANT TO SKIP THIS page, for what I have to tell you is quite disturbing. It is, in my Evil Opinion, the worst news I could ever imagine.

Cavies are on the menu in Peru!

They grill us, bake us, and put us into stews. They sauté, baste, and fricassee us. Oh, the horror! This must be stopped. When I take over the world, I shall lead a cavy uprising. We will chase all the humans from Peru so that cavies can roam free and not

worry about ending up on someone's plate.

Until that time, I shall keep a safe distance from the Elderly One. She is not to be trusted. There is a hungry look in her eyes.

But there is more bad news. After Elliot carried me outside, I watched helplessly as the canine found the order form for Thor's Hammer. Right before my eyes, he thwarted my Evil Plan. He destroyed the form by covering it in slobber and dirt. He is cleverer than I thought. Well, well, well, it appears he has thrown down the gauntlet. Challenge accepted! He thinks he has saved himself from a bonk on the head, but he has underestimated me. I will make a new plan for his elimination—a plan so genius, his simple doggy brain will not be able to comprehend. Victory shall be mine!

JASMINE: Jackson and I are going swimming. Can Gizmo come with us?

ELLIOT: In the pool?

JASMINE: Sure. He can use Barbie's raft.
Come on. It'll be fun!

MOM: Put Wedgie inside. I don't want
him running around the pool again
and falling in.

Jasmine grabs the canine by the collar and pulls him into the house. Then she closes the door. Elliot follows Jasmine to the backyard. I have not yet visited this area. I wonder if I will see any places that might work for my lair? I perch in Elliot's hand, trying to get a good view. We stop at the edge of a huge pool of water. How very interesting. The water is sky blue. It sparkles in the sunshine. Elliot places me upon a floatation device and sets me adrift.

As a species, we cavies are excellent swimmers. I have never been on a raft before. Floating is a very pleasant sensation. Whilst I stretch on my belly, the three human children play in the water. The canine is watching us from the window, drooling with envy. I wave at him. That's right, Thorgi, I see you. You tried to stop me from ordering Thor's Hammer, but I will come up with another Evil Plan. For I am an Evil Genius, and I shall still defeat you! Then I turn away from him and that is when I observe something most interesting.

JASMINE: Jackson, why are you making that weird face? Are you peeing?

JACKSON: Uh-huh.

MOM: Jackson, that's bad. You're not supposed to pee in the pool.

ELLIOT: Gross. Does he do that a lot?

MOM: No, just this one time, right, Jackson?

JACKSON: I peed in the pool one thousand times!

ELLIOT: AAHH!

A thousand pees? I'm never going in there again.

JASMINE: The pool is poisoned!

What turn of events is this? The beautiful blue water has suddenly become poisonous, and the humans will no longer swim in it. How interesting. I do not possess the Hammer of Thor, but another excellent opportunity has presented itself. Somehow, I will lure the canine into the

Pool of a Thousand Pees, where he will meet his doom. I shall be free of his pokey nose and build my Evil Lair. My archenemy will be vanquished!

Muh-ha-ha!

CHAPTER 14

Wedgie

I'M INSIDE. MOM, ELLIOT, JASMINE, JACKSON,
and the Furry Potato are outside.

I want to play with my pack. Why can't I
play with my pack?

CHAPTER 15

Gizmo

IT IS MORNING, DEAR READER. MY BELLY FEELS much better and I am ready to begin my Evil Work again. I decide to focus on my Evil Plan, but a creaking sound draws my attention. The human girl is tiptoeing into Elliot's room. And she is heading straight for the Barbie Playhouse. Oh, drat.

Why must she continue to bother me? I shudder when I spy the object in her hand— the dreaded Biju Ting Ting Scalp Massager. I try to hide in Barbie's pink closet, but the girl grabs me and puts the Biju Ting Ting on top of my head. It makes every muscle in my body relax. I cannot move. I begin to feel sleepy. How very annoying. Does she not realize what important work I have to do? She giggles. Does she think it is funny to immobilize me? What a fiendish child! She kisses my head, then hurries away. Good riddance.

Finally, I am left in peace. I turn my attention to my list. Over the last few days, it has grown much longer.

MY EVIL PLAN

1. Escape the pink prison and build an Evil Genius Lair.
2. Get rid of Thorgi.
3. Get rid of the Elderly One.
4. Get rid of the Biju Ting Ting Scalp Massager.
5. Make pink hearts, green clovers, and yellow stars the official food of all cavies.
6. Become the king of all cavies, create a cavy uprising, and take over the world!

Oh, double drat! The girl is back. I squeak at her to go away, but she does not obey.

She kisses my head again, then she slides a sparkly tutu around my middle. True, the blue of the garment does compliment my eyes. And true, I have a pleasingly large rump that looks good in ruffles. But I do not have time to model her clothing. Does she not see my appointment list? I have a very full schedule!

ELLIOT: Jasmine, what are you doing in
my room?
JASMINE: I wanted to see Gizmo.
ELLIOT: You put him in that tutu
again? I told you not to dress
him up.
JASMINE: But...
ELLIOT: Stop coming in here and bugging
him. And stop bugging me!

Elliot closes his bedroom door. The girl is gone. Elliot removes the sparkly tutu from my midsection and throws it across the

room. He is a loyal servant. He understands
the importance of my work.

ELLIOT: I'm sorry, Gizmo. (sigh)
I'm sorry we moved here. I miss my
old friends.

Elliot is sad. I wonder if there is anything
I might do to cheer him up. Perhaps if I allow
him to clean my litter
box, he will feel happier?
It is an honor, of course,
to clean the litter of
someone as important
as me. I point at the
soiled wood chips,
but Elliot does not
notice. He sits on
the edge of his bed,
his shoulders
hunched.

I understand Elliot's sadness. I too miss old friends. Since the move to this new house, there have been no letters from Gweneviere. What has become of my carrier pigeons? I will need to find new ones. But whenever a bird, be it a robin, a crow, or a pigeon, lands on the windowsill, that drooling canine barks at it and chases it away. Thorgi must be dealt with or, I fear, I will never be able to send another letter to my future queen.

So, the first challenge before me is this—to rid myself of Thorgi. My plan is to lure him into the Pool of a Thousand Pees and be done with him. Genius, of course. Evil Genius.

But how will I achieve this? Over the past few days I have noticed that the canine is easily distracted. When he sees something new, he always goes to sniff it. Sticking his nose where it doesn't belong seems to be his only talent. Therefore, I will lure him with something bright and shiny.

I nibble on alfalfa pellets, waiting for the perfect time to engage my cunning plan.

DAD: Come on, Elliot. We're all going to the beach.

MOM: Elliot, your birthday's tomorrow. Are you excited?

ELLIOT: Not really. It won't be the same without my friends.

JASMINE: But we'll be here.

JACKSON: I love birthday cake!

ELLIOT: I just want to forget about my birthday.

DAD: You don't mean that.

ELLIOT: Yes, I do.

DAD: Okay, everyone, enough standing around. Go grab your bathing suits.

MOM: Wedgie, you'll have to stay here. We aren't going to Dog Beach today.

I sit up. How delightful. The family is going to take a trip, but they will leave the canine behind. There will be no one to save him from his fate. I rub my paws together. This will be so much fun! I listen for the front door to close and for everyone's footsteps to fade. I purr with satisfaction. It is time to show the whole world what an Evil Genius I am!

With a series of jumps, I make my way down the bookcase and onto the carpet. Then I waddle to Elliot's doorway and peer down the hall. The canine stands at the end of the hall, scratching on the front door. He is whimpering. And he is not wearing his cape. I suspect he lost it. What kind of superhero loses his cape? He barks and runs in a circle. Such noise pollution! Once I get rid of him, I shall receive dozens of thank-you cards from the neighbors. In fact, I bet the neighborhood will throw a block party in my honor.

But what is this? I hear more footsteps, slow and shuffling. Horrors! It is the Elderly One. What is she doing here? Why did she not go to the beach with the rest of the humans? She opens the door and lets the canine outside. Then she goes back to her throne. For a moment I am worried. The Elderly One, with her hunger for cooked cavy, is a danger to me. But I will not let her get in my way. Today, my Evil Goal is to lure Thorgi into the Pool of a Thousand Pees. Victory shall be mine!

I venture into Jasmine's room and locate my Polar Expedition Rucksack and water bottle. An Evil Genius must stay hydrated. Then I search the landscape until I find exactly what I am looking for—a piece of blue sea glass. During those days in Jasmine's room, I watched this piece of glass reflect sunlight and cast a blue spot on the wall. When Jasmine picked up the piece of sea glass, the spot moved around. This would certainly distract the canine.

I set the sea glass into my rucksack, sling it onto my back, then make my way down the hall. The canine is outside, barking. I do not have time to build a battering ram, so for now, there is no way for me to open the front door. Thus, I continue into the living room.

The Elderly One is lying on her throne. She has fallen asleep. A bag of cheesy treats is tucked under her arm. Having eaten only alfalfa pellets and water for the last two days, I am overjoyed to see these treats. I stand on my hind legs and stretch my body, making it as long as possible. One of the treats has fallen onto the cushion. How delightful! I grab the orange morsel and dart under the coffee table. My mouth waters as I gaze upon my treasure. Then I sink my teeth into it. I shiver with happiness, for it is delicious!

I consume the treat, then carefully clean

cheesy crumbs from my face. An Evil Genius must always look his best. The canine starts barking again. It is time to deal with him. I crawl out from the coffee table and . . .

jump onto a footstool . . .

jump onto a chair . . .

jump onto a table . . .

jump onto a shelf . . .

then jump onto the windowsill.

After taking a moment to catch my breath, I check over my shoulder to make sure the Elderly One is still asleep. She is. The window provides me with a perfect view. The backyard is green and lush. There is a palm tree and a grapefruit tree. There are roses in bloom. The Pool of a Thousand Pees sparkles in the sunlight. It looks so refreshing and inviting, the canine will never suspect that the water is poisonous.

I remove the sea glass from my rucksack and hold it up to catch a ray of sun.

Then I aim the ray at the cement patio that surrounds the pool. It makes a lovely blue dot. I move the blue dot back and forth. It only takes a few moments for the canine to notice. The barking stops. With a burst of speed, the canine runs toward the dot.

This is going to be easier than I thought. I move the blue dot closer to the pool. The canine tries to catch it with his paws. Then he tries to bite it. I shake my head. How can a brain that is ten times larger than mine be so empty? I move the dot again. Closer and closer. I cannot contain my laughter.

Muh-ha-ha.

Suddenly, the canine skids to a stop. He turns away, distracted.

A white van has pulled into the driveway. A man steps out of the van. The canine forgets about chasing the dot. He wags his tail. That is when I realize that, once again, I have underestimated my archenemy. The words on the side of the van read:

FRED'S POOL CLEANING SERVICE

No! I cry, shaking my fists. Foiled again! The sea glass tumbles to the floor. The canine must have suspected my cunning plan, and thus, he called a cleaning service to remove the poisonous water. The Pool of a Thousand Pees will no longer be toxic. Curse you, Thorgi!

But what is this? I am being lifted into the air. I find myself staring into the watery eyeballs of the Elderly One. And she looks hungry!

CHAPTER **16**

Wedgie

MY FAMILY'S GONE, BUT THE POOL MAN'S here. I LOVE the pool man. Whenever he comes to visit, he always brings me treats. I LOVE treats. I forget all about the funny blue light. I wag and sniff the pool man's ankles. He smells like swimming pool water. Hello, pool man. Can I have a treat?

POOL MAN: Hi, Wedgie. Where's your cape?

Cape is a good word. I LOVE my cape. But my cape's gone. Mom took it away this morning.

MOM: Wedgie, your cape is very dirty. I need to wash it.
Don't worry, Wedgie, you'll get the cape back when it's clean.

I really want to get my cape back. Jasmine gave me the cape. I LOVE Jasmine. I wag as fast as I can and whine, real loud so the pool man can hear me. He sticks his hand into his pocket and pulls out a treat. He reaches down. I grab it from his fingers and swallow it whole. I don't even taste it. I wait for another treat. I get one. I swallow that one whole, too.

The pool man opens his van and pulls out his tools and buckets. He's not petting me, so I run across the yard and press my nose to the fence. I see my stick lying in

Brutus's grass. There are people working in Brutus's yard. Hello, people! Can I have my stick? I ask. But they don't get my stick. I run up and down the fence. Can I have my stick? I ask again. One of the people picks up my stick and puts it onto a pile. Then another person takes the pile and puts it into a truck. Hey! I shout. That's my stick! But they don't hear me because there's a loud noise. A man's pushing a machine that cuts grass. I HATE that machine. It hurts my ears. I run onto the porch and scratch at the front door. No one lets me in. I'm not wearing my cape, so my superpowers don't open the door.

I'm sad. I lie down on the porch.

I wait for the car. I wait for my family. They'll come back. They always come back. Sometimes I worry that they won't come back. I worry that I'll be left alone. I don't like that feeling. I scratch at the door again. But no one lets me in. The pool man leaves.

The yard people leave. My stick's gone. My cape's gone. My family's gone. I put my chin on the ground and wait.

CHAPTER **17**

Gizmo

DEAR READER, **MY LITTLE GUINEA PIG HEART**
is pounding at an alarming speed.

Can you blame me? When faced with a
human who is a hundred times my size and
who likes to eat my species, how can I not be
afraid? From the hungry look in the Elderly
One's eyes, I am clearly on the menu.

I go into survival mode. I kick. I bite. I
squeal. But she is strong for her advanced
years. She holds tight and carries me to the
kitchen. I think for certain that my time has

come. My life flashes before my eyes. The sweet days with my littermates, frolicking in our nest. The lovely days at Swampy's Pet Shop, watching Gweneviere train on her wheel. The glorious days in my old Evil Lair, creating the Evil Blueprints for my future kingdom. Alas, is this how it is going to end? In the Elderly One's stomach?

She sets me onto a counter in the kitchen. Under normal circumstances I would have been overjoyed to be in the presence of so much food. I smell grains, fruits, and green vegetables. But I ignore these scents, because a pot sits on the stove, exactly like the one on that television show. Woe is me! I am overcome with despair. What will the cavy species do without me? How can cavies take over the world without an awesome leader?

I do not blame the Elderly One for wanting to eat me. I am meaty, and I possess a fine round rump. There is no doubt in my mind that I would taste delicious. But my destiny is not to be stewed!

As the Elderly One searches through a drawer, I scurry up and down the counter, but there is no place to hide. The toaster's slots are too narrow, and the blender contains a dangerous blade. If I try to jump off the counter, surely I will be flattened. The Elderly One takes out a long piece of tape. She measures me from nose to tail. She wraps it around my belly and measures my girth. She is measuring me for her cooking pot!

There is only one choice—I must jump! As soon as the Elderly One turns her back, I run, my little legs pumping as fast as they can. Then I jettison myself off the counter . . . landing on a table . . .

I scurry around a vase of flowers . . .

then dive onto a chair . . .

I leap from one chair to another . . .

then jump to the floor.

I make it in one piece!

ABUELA: *Cavia? Where did you go? Cavia?*

She is looking for me. But I know the perfect place to hide. Whilst exploring Elliot's room last night, I discovered a hole behind the trim under his bed. It had been chewed by a mouse. I scamper quickly up the hallway into Elliot's room, then under his bed. The hole is too small for me, so I chew as fast as I can. I can hear the Elderly One calling for me in the kitchen. I chew faster. After a few minutes, I am able to enlarge the hole so I can squeeze through. The Elderly One will have to find someone else to eat!

I settle behind Elliot's wall, my little heart still pounding. What a day this has been. Thorgi escaped the Pool of a Thousand Pees, and I escaped the Elderly One. I will stay here for a while. Until it is safe to come out.

But I am hungry. Until further notice, please send your care packages to me at:

Gizmo the Evil Genius
Behind the Wall in Elliot's Room
Nowhere Near the Andes Mountains

CHAPTER **18**

Wedgie

WHAT'S THAT? IT'S THE CAR! I JUMP TO MY paws. My family's back! I'm so happy! When they get out of the car, I smell Jasmine's ankles. They smell like sand and lotion. She pats my head. I smell Jackson's ankles. They smell like salt water. I lick them. Hello, people! I've been alone all day! Pet me pet me pet me! Everyone pets me, except for Elliot. I run around him, wagging, but he still doesn't pet me.

We go inside. I smell everyone's shoes.

I lick Jackson's hand. I roll on my back and get some belly scratches from my new dad. I LOVE belly scratches.

ELLIOT: Where's Gizmo?

    DAD: He's not in your room?

ELLIOT: No. I can't find him.

Uh-oh. Something's wrong. Elliot sounds upset. Dad stops scratching me. What did I do? I don't hear any important words like *get*, *stop*, or *don't*. No one's talking to me. They're looking around. Jasmine's looking under the couch. Mom's looking in the pantry. Dad lifts the lid on the toilet and looks inside. Are we playing a game?

JASMINE: Abuela? Where's Gizmo?

ABUELA: Who?

JASMINE: Elliot's guinea pig.

ABUELA: I don't know. He ran off.

ELLIOT: Ran off?

ABUELA: He was sitting at the window.
He was trying to make the dog
fall into the pool.

ELLIOT: What's she talking about?

MOM: I'm sure Gizmo is fine. Let's all look
for him.

Yes, we're playing a game. But what are we looking for? I wag my stubby tail. I wanna play!

We keep looking. We look everywhere.

Are we looking for my cape? I would like to find my cape. Let's find my cape! Jasmine and Jackson are looking. Mom and Dad are looking. Elliot's looking too. I find lots of things. There are dirty socks under Jackson's bed. There's a tiny shell on Jasmine's shoe. There's something moldy between the wall and the cold food machine, but I can't get it.

DAD: Are we sure we checked every room?

JASMINE: Yes. Twice!

ELLIOT: What if he got outside?

MOM: Abuela, did you accidentally let Elliot's guinea pig outside?

ABUELA: In Peru, they are very happy to live outside.

ELLIOT: He can't go outside. He might get hit by a car!

We all run outside to look for my cape. We look in the bushes. We look under the porch. I piddle on the hedge. I chase a squirrel up Squirrel Tree. I run over to the fence. Brutus! Did you take my cape? Give me my cape! I'm very mad at Brutus. He should stop taking my stuff. I piddle on the fence. Brutus doesn't say anything.

A truck pulls up. A man gets out. He's holding balloons. I don't like balloons. They float up in the air and then they explode. I don't like that sound.

DELIVERY MAN: Are you the birthday boy?

ELLIOT: Not until tomorrow.

DELIVERY MAN: Well, I guess you get to celebrate a day early.

DAD: Oh look, Elliot. The balloons are from Grandpa.

ELLIOT: I don't want to celebrate early. Not without Gizmo.

Elliot sounds very sad. He runs back into the house. This is Brutus's fault. I stick my nose into Brutus's yard. I whimper. Brutus? Where's my cape? Please give me my cape so Elliot won't be sad. Elliot wants me to be Super Wedgie again.

But Brutus just stares at me.

CHAPTER **19**

Gizmo

DEAR READER, I SPEND THE REST OF THE DAY behind the wall. The humans search for me, but their efforts are in vain. The canine follows them around, but he does not find me either. I am not a lowly farm animal to be herded. I am Gizmo the Evil Genius, and no creature shall find me unless I want to be found!

But hunger is a powerful force. I am tempted to dash into the kitchen and snatch an apple. Or burrow beneath the couch pillows for one of those cheesy treats. But I must stay hidden, for if I emerge in daylight, I might end up in the Elderly One's cooking pot. Fortunately, the mouse who once lived in this hole has left an acorn. It is withered, and not very tasty, but it will hold me over.

Surely Elliot does not know the Elderly One's plans. He is my loyal servant and he would never allow me to be cooked. I need to tell Elliot the truth. So, when the humans go back outside, I scurry out of the hole and toss a note onto Elliot's pillow.

> The Elderly One wants to eat me!

Then, just as the humans return, I dart back into my hiding place.

I hear Elliot's footsteps. He will read the note and tell the others. Then the Elderly One will be sent away. But when I peer from the hole, I see the canine sitting on the floor beside the bed, eating my note! How dare he! I will no longer be fooled by the dumb expression on the canine's face. He is more cunning than he looks, and his very purpose in life is to thwart me and my Evil Plans.

ELLIOT: Dad, do you think Gizmo ran away? Do you think he's mad because he's stuck in the Barbie Playhouse?

DAD: I don't think a guinea pig cares about things like that. Besides, his new cage will be delivered soon.

ELLIOT: Maybe he doesn't like it here. Maybe he doesn't want to be my pet anymore.

DAD: Gizmo loves you. He didn't run away. He's just exploring. It'll be okay. Go to sleep. We'll search again tomorrow.

I do not want Elliot to worry about me. But until I have gotten rid of the Elderly

One, I can't let anyone find me.

The lights go out, and the house grows quiet. Elliot stops tossing and turning and his breathing slows. He is asleep. The canine snores from his basket in the living room. It is time to put my Evil Plan into motion. I leave my hiding place. What's this? Elliot has placed my food dish on the carpet. He knew I'd be hungry. What a good servant he is. But when I look inside, the dish is empty and covered in dog slobber. That thief! Stealing my precious alfalfa pellets! I will have my revenge! My belly growls. Despite my hunger, I must press on. There is much to do.

I find a piece of paper and pen and I write a shipping label for the human who collects the mail. It reads:

Attention Mail Delivery Human:
Return this Elderly One to Peru.
Special Overnight Airmail Delivery.
First Class. Right Away. Do Not Delay!

I tuck the label into my Polar Expedition Rucksack. Unfortunately, my water bottle is empty. I sling the rucksack onto my back. I cross the hallway and enter a room I have not yet explored. It belongs to the Elderly One. She is sleeping in her nest. I jump onto a stool, then onto her nest. Very slowly, I walk up her pillow. Her eyes are closed. There are strange orange rods all over her head. I take the delivery label and stick it onto her forehead. In the morning, the mail

delivery human will come and take the Elderly One away, to ship her to Peru. Sometimes I am amazed by my own brilliance. I rub my paws together with glee.

The night is just getting started.

I peer down the hallway to make certain the coast is clear, then I waddle into Jasmine's room. It only takes a few minutes to find that which I seek. The Biju Ting Ting Scalp Massager lies on the carpet next to a tablet of paper and crayons. A picture has been drawn on the tablet. It appears to be a potato with fur, stick legs, and glasses. How odd. I hope Jasmine does not want to be an artist when she grows up, because this drawing is terrible. There is no such thing as a furry potato.

But there is no time to ponder Jasmine's future, for I have work to do. I turn my attention to the Biju Ting Ting. With my sharp teeth, I begin to chew my way through its pieces. Never again will it be used to immobilize me! I quickly turn it into a pile of little pieces. I grab one of Jasmine's socks. I place the little pieces into the sock. Then I start walking backward down the hallway, pulling the sock with my teeth.

I bump right into the canine's basket. He is still fast asleep, his legs twitching. I smile most Evilly, for little does he know, he will soon be in trouble. Big, big trouble. That is what he deserves for eating my food, destroying my notes, and getting in my way. Thorgi, you shall feel my wrath!

One by one, I set the pieces of the Biju Ting Ting Scalp Massager into his basket, ever so careful not to wake him. When I am finished, I pause to savor the moment. Jasmine will think that her canine destroyed her precious toy. She will get so upset, she will banish the canine from this home. How clever I am! I want to laugh with Evil Glee, but I clap my paws over my mouth so as not to wake anyone.

In a single night, I have defeated my three foes—the Biju Ting Ting Scalp Massager, the Elderly One, and Thorgi. Good riddance to all of you!

But, until the Elderly One has been mailed to Peru, I must continue to hide. And so, I make my way back to the hole in

Elliot's wall. I feel a bit dizzy as I waddle. A bit weak. I need something to eat, but alas, I find not a crumb along the way.

Hopefully, the morning will bring a bright new day, a day without the Biju Ting Ting, without the Elderly One, and without the canine. And then, I shall be free to build my Evil Lair.

Tomorrow will be glorious!

CHAPTER 20

Wedgie

I'M A BAD DOG. I DON'T KNOW WHY. *BAD DOG*, Jasmine tells me. *Bad Dog*, she says again. Jasmine won't pet me. She's frowning at me. She's stomping her foot.

> **JASMINE:** Mom! Wedgie chewed up my scalp massager!
> **MOM:** Oh no. Bad Wedgie.
> **JASMINE:** Yes. Bad dog!

I don't like the word *bad*. I don't want to be bad. How did all these things get into my basket? I don't remember putting them here. And why do they smell like the Furry Potato?

JASMINE: Go away, Wedgie, I'm mad at you.

MOM: Jasmine, I want you to put a smile on your face. It's Elliot's birthday today.

JASMINE: Okay. But I'm still mad at Wedgie.

I lie on the floor and whimper. I am a bad dog, and I don't know why. My family walks into the kitchen and sits at the table. It's breakfast time. I smell waffles. I LOVE waffles. I slink into the kitchen and wait next to Jackson's chair. I know that Jackson will drop a piece of waffle. He always drops things for me. He LOVES me. I sit quietly. And wait. And wait. Where is the waffle? Please oh please oh please give me a piece of waffle. But I am a bad dog, so I don't get a waffle.

DAD:	Did Gizmo come back last night?
ELLIOT:	No. I don't know what to do. What if he's outside?
JASMINE:	We could walk around the neighborhood and ask the neighbors if they've seen him.
MOM:	That's a good idea.
DAD:	Do you have a photo of Gizmo for the posters?
ELLIOT:	Just a baby photo.
JASMINE:	I have something that will work!

Everyone's moving around. They're busy. They don't pet me. What's going on? Dad's carrying my leash. He puts it on me. He wants me to take him for a walk. But where's my cape? I sure miss my cape. I'm not Super Wedgie without my cape.

Mom and Abuela wave good-bye as Dad,

Elliot, Jasmine, Jackson, and I go outside for a walk. I start heading toward Duck Pond, but Dad tugs on my leash. We stop at a neighbor's house. Elliot knocks on the door. The door opens. I sniff the neighbor's ankles. They smell like dust and cat. Is there a cat inside this house? I narrow my eyes.

JASMINE: Hi, Mr. Schwartz. This is my new brother, Elliot. His pet is missing.

ELLIOT: Have you seen him? His name is Gizmo.

MR. SCHWARTZ: Well, my cat killed a mouse last night. Is Gizmo a mouse?

ELLIOT: No, he's a guinea pig.

MR. SCHWARTZ: Haven't seen him.

ELLIOT: What if a cat gets Gizmo?

DAD: Don't worry. We'll keep looking.

This is a very long walk. We stop at another house, then another. There are so many ankles to sniff. Some smell like soap.

Some smell like socks. Some of the neighbors pet me. *Hello, Wedgie*, they say. *Where's your cape*? I don't know where my cape is. I really want my cape. At each house, there are ankles to smell and new plants to piddle on. I press my nose against Jasmine's leg. She doesn't pet me. Am I still a bad dog?

We've walked the entire neighborhood and now we're going home. But Dad stops at Brutus's house. Brutus is lying in his yard, next to the fence. I growl. Stay away from my family, Brutus! Dad drops my leash and he, Elliot, Jasmine, and Jackson walk up the porch and knock on Brutus's door. Leaving me in the yard with Brutus. Brutus lifts his head and looks at me. He sees that I don't have my cape. He sees that I am not Super Wedgie. Will he attack? I stand my ground. Brutus gets up and walks toward me. He sure is slow. It takes him a long, long time. I try to look fierce. But he's a very big dog. When I look up, all I see are his legs and his belly. He sniffs me. Then, he wags his tail. I sniff him. Then I wag my stubby tail. We both wag our tails. I walk around him, again and again. We wag and wag and wag. Hey, people! Guess what? Brutus is my friend!

DAD: Elliot! Where are you going?
ELLIOT: We'll never find Gizmo. He's gone! This is the worst birthday ever!

My family is running home. See ya, Brutus! I bound after them, my leash dragging behind me. Why are we running? What's happening?

CHAPTER 21

Gizmo

TODAY WAS NOT GLORIOUS, DEAR READER. The Elderly One is still out there. As is the canine. The only thing I managed to destroy is the Biju Ting Ting Scalp Massager. At least I can cross one thing off my Evil Plan, yet there is so much more to do. I am parched. And famished. An entire day gone by with no water or food. And no one has sent me a care package. An Evil Genius cannot survive on air!

Night has fallen, but I am too tired to

leave this hole and search for food. How can I face my foes if I am weakened by thirst and hunger?

Am I doomed? I did not make Gweneviere my queen. I did not build my new Evil Lair. So many things I wanted to accomplish, and yet, I have not the strength to drag myself from this hiding place. I have never gone this long without something to eat.

Oh, woe is me.

CHAPTER 22

Wedgie

I DON'T LIKE THIS NIGHT. The balloons are tied to a chair in the kitchen. They float and make shadows on the floor. They're super scary. Jasmine's in her room with the door shut. She won't pet me. Elliot's in his room with the door shut. He won't pet me. Mom and Dad and

Abuela are staring at the television screen. Only Jackson will pet me. I lick his face. It tastes like orange juice.

JACKSON: Wedgie, that tickles. Hey, where's your cape?
Mom? Where's Wedgie's cape?
MOM: In the dryer.

I hear the word *cape*. I wag my stub. Yes, I want my cape. Do you have my cape? I follow Jackson down the hall, to the Warm Room. I like to sleep in the Warm Room. He opens something and pulls out . . . MY CAPE! I bark with joy. Jackson found my cape! I LOVE Jackson.

I'm so happy I can't stop wiggling. My front end and my back end are both moving. My paws make clicking sounds on the floor. I was sad but now I'm happy. Happy, happy, happy! Jackson found my cape!

He ties it around my neck. I feel different. I feel like . . . Super Wedgie.

I run down the hall and scratch on

Jasmine's door. Look, Jasmine, I'm Super
Wedgie again! I run across the hall and
scratch on Elliot's door. Look, Elliot, I'm
Super Wedgie again! I run in circles, activat-
ing my superpowers, and the door opens!

JACKSON: Elliot? Don't you want birthday cake?

ELLIOT: No.

I want Gizmo to come back.

I run up to the Furry Potato's cage. Look, Furry Potato, I'm . . .

Hey, where's the Furry Potato? Did he get lost again? That silly Furry Potato. Don't worry, people. Now that I have my cape, I'll find him. I'll find him with my superpowers of smell and my superpowers of sight. Here I come, Furry Potato. Super Wedgie to the rescue!

I sniff around the room until I find a little trail. A little trail made by tiny paws. I find a tiny Furry Potato poop. It tastes good. I find another tiny Furry Potato poop. The trail leads under Elliot's bed. I sniff and sniff. The trail moves around a shoe, and over a book, and stops at the wall. I press my nose to the wall. The smell is stronger in this place. I scratch at the wall. I bark and bark and bark.

    ELLIOT: Hey, Wedgie, stop that. Get out of
                  my room!
       DAD: What's he doing under your bed?
    ELLIOT: He's barking at something.
       DAD: Let's see what it is.

I stick my nose into the hole, as far as it will go. Hey, it smells like the Furry Potato. My nose touches something furry. Yes, it's the Furry Potato. What are you doing, Furry

Potato? Are you sleeping? Wake up, Furry Potato. I'm Super Wedgie again!

DAD: There's a hole back here.

JACKSON: Can I see?

ELLIOT: It's Gizmo!

JASMINE: What's the matter with him? Why isn't he moving?

JACKSON: Is he dead?

Dad carries Gizmo into the kitchen and puts him on the counter. I can't see. I stand on my back legs but I still can't see. What's going on up there? I lick my lips. I wonder if I can find more Furry Potato poop?

JASMINE: Look, he's moving.

MOM: He's eating! He's going to be okay!

DAD: I think we found him just in time.

JACKSON: Wedgie found him.

ELLIOT: You're right. Wedgie found him.

Elliot gets on his knees. Hello, Elliot. What are you doing down here on the floor? He hugs me. And pets me. And kisses my face. He's smiling. I'm so happy that Elliot's smiling. I wag my tail. I LOVE Elliot.

Then Jasmine gets down on the floor and she hugs me. And pets me. And kisses my face. I LOVE Jasmine. I wag so fast it starts to hurt. I run in circles. Round and round Elliot. Round and round Jasmine. Everyone pets me. I'm so happy.

JASMINE: I'm sorry I called you a bad dog.
ELLIOT: Thank you for finding Gizmo.
You're the best dog ever.
And this is the best birthday
ever.
EVERYONE: Happy birthday, Elliot!

CHAPTER 23

Gizmo

HELLO AGAIN, DEAR READER.

You will be pleased to learn that I am fully recovered from what was nearly a deadly case of dehydration and starvation. But I am back, and in full health, and as determined as ever to complete my Evil Plan.

But first, a bit of news. Whilst I was enjoying a snack of carrot stick and broccoli stalk, Elliot walked into his room with a large package in hand.

ELLIOT: Look, it finally came!
It's your new Eco Habitat.
JASMINE: That's a really nice cage. Gizmo
seems very happy.

I spend the afternoon exploring my new home. Just like my old Eco Habitat, there is a tunnel system, an elimination chamber, and a stellar exercise wheel. But this

new model comes with a few upgrades—
it is larger and the nesting chamber is
soundproof, which will be nice because the
canine is very noisy.

So, I'm pleased to report that I have a
new address. You may send your letters and
care packages to me at:

Gizmo the Evil Genius
The Eco Habitat
The Bookshelf in Elliot's Room
Nowhere Near the Andes Mountains

As I waddle on my wheel, I think about
all the things that have happened. I over-
heard the humans say that the canine saved
my life. I do not know if this is true, for I
was unconscious at the time of my discovery. And I have no further comment on this.

Except to say that I am considering moving him from Enemy #1 on my list to Enemy #2. I shall think more on this subject and let you know what I decide.

The Postal Service did not send the Elderly One back to Peru. She removed the shipping label from her forehead before the postal delivery human arrived. She may have outsmarted me this time, but I will find a way to be rid of her. Elliot tells me that he is happy I didn't run away. He is doing a good job as my servant. I am confident that he will not allow the Elderly One to cook me. But still, I must be wary in her presence.

I am about to take a nap, but Elliot picks me up and carries me down the hall. Are we going in search of a new treat? As we pass by an open door, I catch a glimpse of something that makes my little heart go pitter-patter. This new human house has a Maytag dryer!

MOM: Look, Elliot. Abuela made your birthday cake.

ELLIOT: Wow, it looks just like Gizmo.

ABUELA: Yes, I measured him to get the cake exactly right.

ELLIOT: Thank you.

DAD: And you thought Abuela might want to eat Gizmo.

ABUELA: Why would I eat Gizmo? I'm a vegetarian.

Well, well, well, now that is an interesting turn of events. It would appear that the Elderly One is afraid of me after all. She knows that if she mistreats me, I will have her shipped back to Peru. So, to keep me happy, she has decided to stop eating meat. I am victorious!

As I sit on Elliot's lap, I ponder the past, present, and future. Now that Elliot has resumed his role as my servant, and I am settled into my new house, I can focus on my new Evil Lair. Tonight, whilst the humans sleep, I will begin building it behind the Maytag dryer. It will be extraordinary.

The future is bright with possibility, dear reader. For the glorious day will come when I, Gizmo the Evil Genius, will become the king of all cavies, create a cavy uprising, and take over the world!

JASMINE: Look, Gizmo. I got a new one.

CHAPTER 24

Wedgie

IT'S A NICE DAY. THE SUN IS SHINING. THE birds are singing. And I have my cape. Look at me, Brutus! I have my cape!

Elliot asks me if I want a stick. Yes, I want a stick! I really want a stick! He grabs a branch off Squirrel Tree and gives it to me. I've got a stick. You see this, Brutus? I got a new stick!

Mom brings my leash. She wants me to take her on a walk. Dad wants to walk. And Jackson wants to walk. And so does Elliot.

And Jasmine wants to walk. What's that in her pocket? Oh, it's the Furry Potato. He wants to walk too. I sniff him all over. He grunts at me. He LOVES me. And I LOVE him. Come on, everyone. Let's all go for a walk.

Super Wedgie's on duty, day or night, night or day, to protect the pack, come what may!

Acknowledgments

STORIES COME TO LIFE IN MANY DIFFERENT ways. In this particular case, an editor named Melissa Miller had a story idea about two odd little characters—a guinea pig named Gizmo and a corgi named Wedgie. But she needed a writer to bring them to life. So she called me, and over the course of a year, we brainstormed, and schemed, and wrote, but mostly, we laughed. And hence you now hold this book in your hands.

Thank you, Melissa, for the opportunity to tap into your imagination and play in this new world. And huge thanks for choosing Barbara to be the illustrator. Barbara, your drawings make me giddy with happiness. You are an equal partner in breathing life into this story. Thank you for getting my humor and for translating it in such a lovely way.

As with every book, there is a team of creative people who work behind the scenes. At Harper Collins/Katherine Tegen Books, that team includes my soccer-loving and adventure-seeking new editor, Maria Barbo. It also includes Kelsey Horton, Rebecca Aronson, David Curtis, Amy Ryan, Jessica Berg, Stephanie Hoover, and Meaghan Finnerty. Thank you everyone for your hard work, dedication, and support!

And on the home front, my personal team includes Michael Bourret, agent extraordinaire, Isabelle Ranson and Walker Ranson, my children and my first readers, and Bob, my rock, my cheerleader, my husband. Love you all!

hands. I look into the watery eyes of the Elderly One. She smiles at me, then carries me to the living room, where she settles onto her throne. It is television-watching time. How lovely. The Elderly One presents me with a cheese puff. It is delicious.

New Evil Plan: I will get rid of Thorgi and the Toof later today. Right now, it's time to nourish my Evil Brain.

Wedgie

I'M SO HAPPY BECAUSE FUNNY DOG IS HERE. She likes to go for walks. She likes to roll on smelly things. But most of all, she likes to dig, just like me. We are digging a hole. We are best friends. I LOVE Funny Dog!

Bestselling author **SUZANNE SELFORS** lives on a mysterious island in the Pacific Northwest, where she spends most of her time making up stories, which is her very favorite thing to do. She has a dog, a cat, and is seriously considering getting an Evil Genius guinea pig.

You can visit her at
www.suzanneselfors.com.

BARBARA FISINGER is an illustrator, character designer, and visual development artist.

You can visit her on Tumblr at
www.barbarafisinger. tumblr.com.

Gizmo

WAIT AN EVIL MINUTE. IF THORGI AND THE royal pig are working together, that can only mean one thing—the pig has become Thorgi's sidekick. Of course! All superheroes have a sidekick. Thorgi and the Toof are in cahoots!

I rub my furry chin. So this is my archenemy's plan. He got himself a sidekick. He believes that two against one will give him a better chance to defeat me. Like Batman and Robin. Or like Han Solo and Chewbacca. He is mistaken!

I shall vanquish them both!

I am about to concoct a new Evil Plan when two human hands reach down and scoop me up. They are wrinkled, spotted

TURN THE PAGE FOR
A SNEAK PEEK AT

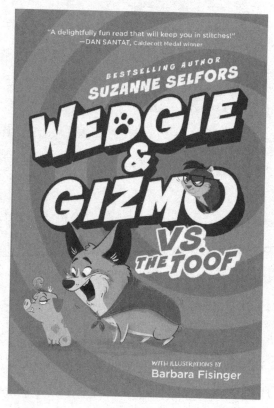

"A delightfully fun read that will keep you in stitches!"
—DAN SANTAT, Caldecott Medal winner

BESTSELLING AUTHOR
SUZANNE SELFORS

WEDGIE
&
GIZMO
VS. THE TOOF

WITH ILLUSTRATIONS BY
Barbara Fisinger